For My Boys

Molly Vidas
Ogre Toes

Story by: Molly Vidas

Art by: Alexandra Kusick

Page and Cover Design by: Teresa Penas

A CIP record for this book is available from the Library of Congress Cataloging-in-Publication Data

Library of Congress Control Number: 9780999552032
ISBN-13: 978-0-9995520-3-2 (hard cover)
ISBN-13: 978-0-9995520-4-9 (soft cover)

It was bedtime. And as Max climbed over the covers and on to his bed, his mother noticed his bare feet and toes.

"Oh my," she said with a smile, "those are some long toenails. Let's cut them before bed."

"No!" Max shouted, and furrowed his brows and crossed his arms.

"Okay," she said, "But if you don't cut your nails, everybody knows you'll get ... "

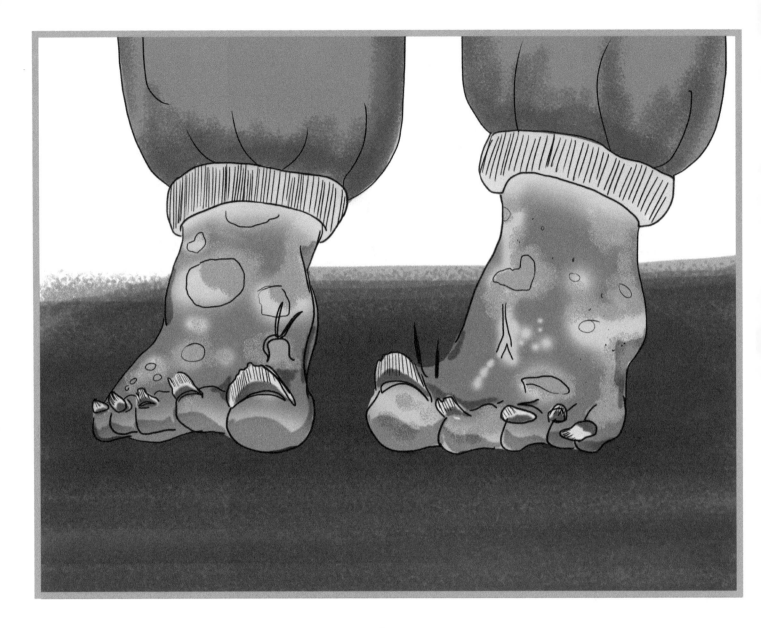

OGRE TOES

"Ogre toes that are **long,** **green**, and **wrinkly.**

You won't be able to wear sandals! So, let's cut your nails."

"No!" yelled Max once more, and this time he covered his feet with his hands.

"Okay ... " she said again, "But if you don't cut your nails, everybody knows you'll get ogre toes. And ogre toes turn in to ... "

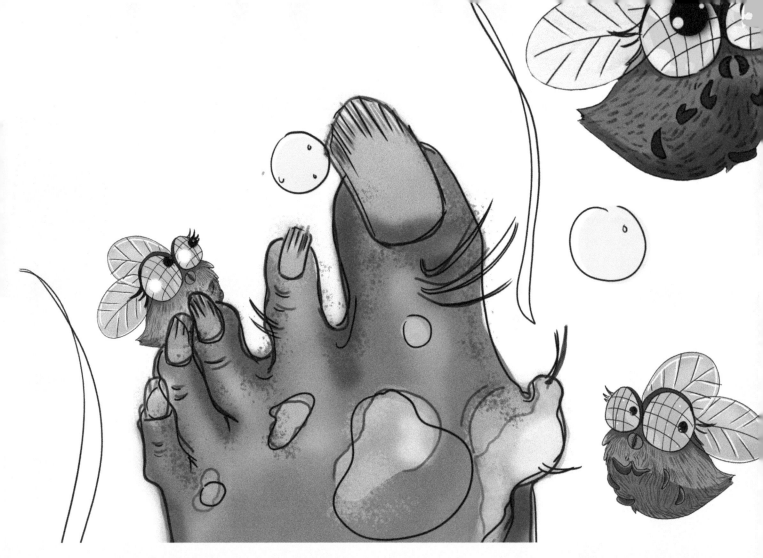

" ... ogre feet! Hairy, smelly, bumpy, **green** ogre feet. None of your shoes will fit! Ogre toes on ogre feet!"

"So ... let's cut your nails."
And what did Max say? ...

"No!" and he crossed his legs and hid his feet under him.

"Okay" said his mom, "but if you don't cut your nails, everybody knows you'll get ogre toes on ogre feet. And ogre feet are part of ...

... OGRE LEGS!

heavy, hairy, crooked

ogre legs.

Ogre legs can't run
fast or jump high.
Ogre toes, on ogre
feet, on ogre legs.

So ... let's cut
your nails."

"No." Max pouted, and he tucked his feet under his blankets.

"Okay," said his mom "but if you don't cut your nails, everybody knows you'll get ogre toes, on ogre feet, on ogre legs. And ogre legs are part of ...

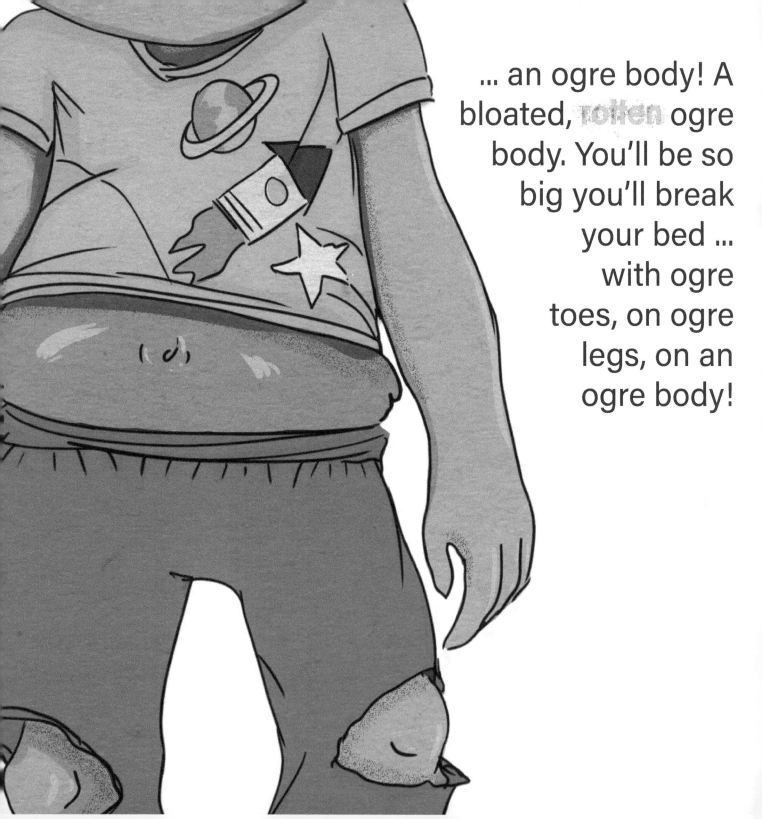

... an ogre body! A bloated, rotten ogre body. You'll be so big you'll break your bed ... with ogre toes, on ogre legs, on an ogre body!

So ... let's cut your nails."
"No!" whined Max quietly, and he hugged a
pillow on his lap.

"Okay," his mom said "but if you don't cut your nails, everybody knows you'll get ...

... ogre toes, on ogre feet, on ogre legs, on an ogre body with ...

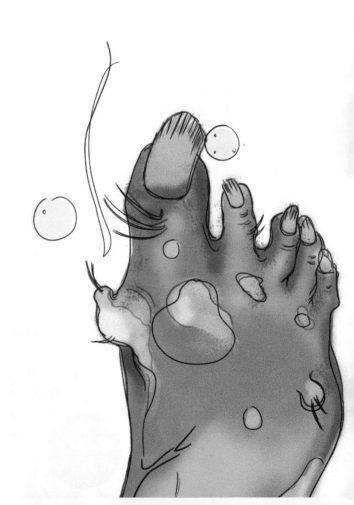

... an ogre head! A large, **lumpy**, uneven ogre head. Your baseball hats won't fit! Ogre toes, on ogre legs, on an ogre body, with an ogre head!

So ... let's cut your nails." This time Max whispered, "No," and hid his whole body under the covers.

"Okay," his mom said once more, "but if you don't cut your nails, everybody knows you'll get ogre toes, on ogre feet ...

... on ogre **legs**, on an ogre **body**, with an ogre **head** that has ...

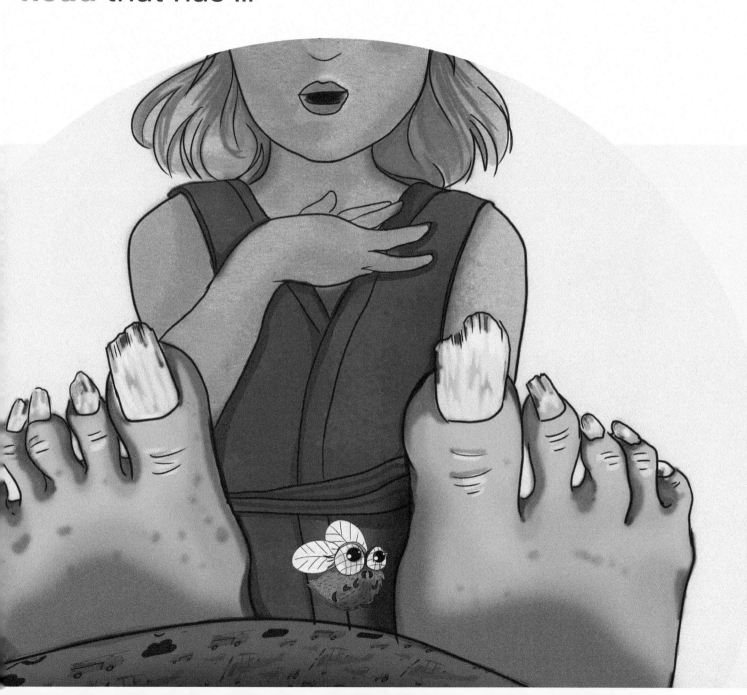

... ogre teeth! Nasty, rotten ogre teeth that can only chew sticks and mud.

Ogre toes, on ogre feet, on ogre legs, on an ogre body with an ogre head and ogre teeth.

And do you know what ogre teeth CAN'T do?" his mom asked.

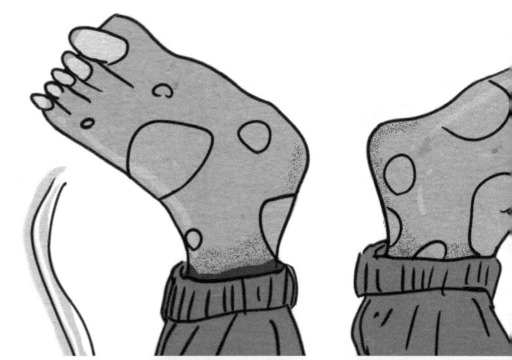

Max slowly peeked from under his covers.

"What?" he asked softly.

His mom smiled, and responded "Ogre teeth can't eat ...

"Candy!"

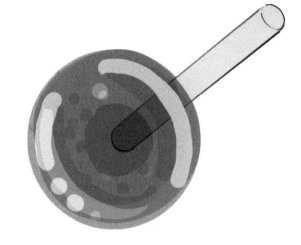

Max threw off his covers.

"Candy?

I like candy! Mama -

Let's cut my nails right now!"

The end

OGRE TOES

This story was created and written for my two boys, Desmond and Isaac, as a way to remember and share one of our family's many silly things. Just like Max, they never wanted to let me cut their toenails, and doing so was always a fight - until the concept of "ogre toes" came to be!

-Molly

Lightning Source UK Ltd.
Milton Keynes UK
UKHW050724061020
371049UK00004B/63